I0749183

Leah and Aya the Sewing Doll

Among other Fairy Tales
by Nargisa Karasartova

Published by Hertfordshire Press Ltd © 2022
e-mail: publisher@hertfordshirepress.com
www.hertfordshirepress.com

Leah and Aya the Sewing Doll,

Among other Fairy Tales by Nargisa Karasartova ©

English

Translator - Nargisa Karasartova
Illustrator - Svetlana Nasunbatova
Editor - Timur Akhmedjanov
Typeset - Alexandra Rey

British Library Catalogue in Publication Data
A catalogue record for this book is available from the British Library
Library of Congress in Publication Data
A catalogue record for this book has been requested

ISBN: 978-1-913356-45-3

CONTENTS

OCA MAGAZINE

BUILDING THE LANDBRIDGE WITH EURASIA

ABOUT OCA MAGAZINE AWARD

The Eurasian Creative Guild (London) presents to your attention an OCA Magazine Award of $5,000 for the best work in the "Publicism" genre, all in the framework of the "Open Eurasia" contest. However, you might be wondering, what is the OCA Magazine?

The OCA Magazine is a quarterly and independent magazine, published in London since 2009 by the Silk Road Media Group with the support of Eurasian Creative Guild (London). It is aimed at English speaking audiences and those who are interested in or are residents of the countries of the former USSR and the Eurasian region. The magazine reports on events from outstanding personalities of the Eurasian region (past and present) and the successful projects of international co-operation in Eurasia. It promotes the cultures, politics, events and communities of both regions and encourages a discussion and exchange of ideas between them to develop both business co-operation, tourist activity and cultural relations.

The guests of the magazine are typically diplomats, politicians and cultural workers from CIS and Europe. Previous issues have presented interviews and articles about: the President of Tatarstan, Mintimer Shaimiev, the President of Kyrgyzstan, Almazbek Atambaev, the leader of the Uzbekistan Liberal Democratic Party, Aktam Khaitov, the leader of the Georgian Labour Party, Shalva Natelashvili, the Russian special envoy for international cultural cooperation, Mikhail Shvydkoy, the culture minister of Tajikistan, Sirojiddin Aslov, the Director of the EBRD office in Tokyo, Masaru Honma and the Moldovan composer, Eugen Doga, as well as many others.

The grant will go on to publication by the publishing house Hertfordshire Press, as part of the ECG Academy series. Thanks to this award, for which quality and professionalism are the main standards, five popular science books of Guild members have already been published and presented around the world.

A fairy tale is the gold that glitters in children's eyes.
Hans Christian Andersen

Fairy tales accompany a person throughout life and history in general. They are told to children from birth, and then they tell them to their children. Fairy tales are a big casket that keeps the traditions, customs, history and way of thinking of a certain era - the experience of ancestors, advice, instructions and warnings for posterity. In this book, the author added unusual and overseas stones to the fabulous casket, which shimmeringly complement the treasury of Kyrgyz national fairy tales, reflecting the truth of life and expressing hope for a wonderful and bright future.

Writer, translator, member of ECG - Elena Bosler-Guseva

Together with the heroes of Nargisa Karasartova's fairy tales, you make an exciting journey, which is sometimes full of dangers and intricacies, but you always discover something new, unknown, and upon returning from the journey, you become stronger and smarter. The generosity of the heart and the indefatigable imagination of the author allow us to plunge into fabulous waves, whether air, sea or otherwise, in order to become more beautiful and purer in soul. Tales of Karasartova Nargisa are filled with goodness and beautiful thoughts. In the works of the author there is no moralism, the imposition of her opinion, the author teaches goodness subtly and filigree. The author's speech is colorful, poetic. The position of the author is always positive, the author's view of certain things is new and fresh.

Poet, writer, member of the National Writers' Union of Kyrgyzstan - Leyla Karasartova

---

Tales of Karasartova Nargisa are always interesting and pleasant to read, you get a special aesthetic pleasure. Reading the fairy tales of Nargisa, you are immersed in an incredibly beautiful world that plays with different colors and shades, and the plot is so intriguing and captures you that you read excitedly to find out what the end of this or that fairy tale will be, the author's ending is always unpredictable and unexpected.

Writer, member of the National Writers' Union of Kyrgyzstan, Excellence in Public Culture in Kyrgyzstan - Shoistai Ravshan

---

Fairy tales by Nargisa Karasartova are liked by adults and children. According to one friend, her son refused to sleep until she read him the fairy tale "The Dolphin Boy" for the night, so he liked it. And another acquaintance said that his grandson, under the impression of "Centipede - Ozhka", counted shoes all the time. I can say that one tale of Nargisa is better than another, since the composition of each individual tale is unique and highly artistic.

Poet, writer, member of the National Writers' Union of Kyrgyzstan, Excellence in Public Culture in Kyrgyzstan, member of ECG – Bubuira Bektenova

Leah and Aya the Sewing Doll

Chapter One

There was once a little girl named Leah who had a lot of toys, out of all her toys, the one she loved the most was her doll named Aya. She was a doll that knew how to think, walk and talk. Though what Aya liked to do more than anything else was to sew cute little things on her little sewing machine.

One summer day, Leah and Aya were playing in the front garden until her mother called the little girl for lunch.

As Leah began to leave, she warned her doll:

"Don't go anywhere now, I'll be back soon."

However, after finishing her lunch the little girl turned on the TV instead and began to watch cartoons, after which she read some books. I must mention that Leah likes to write fairy tales from time to time.

Aya had been waiting for her friend until late in the evening and eventually became quite upset that Leah had forgotten about her. Aya decided that she didn't want to wait any longer, so she picked up her sewing machine and went into the forest.

When it got dark, the little girl looked out of the window and remembered her doll which she left outside, she ran to the garden but she could not find Aya. Saddened by the absence of her dear friend, Leah began to cry.

"Aya, where did you go?! Where are you?!"

Leah was worried after leaving her favorite doll outside for such long time. To comfort her crying daughter, Leah's mother handed her another doll. The little girl gave this doll a different name – Maya, this new friend of hers also knew how to think, walk and talk. She does not sew like Aya did, although she does write down every story thought up by Leah using a little ballpoint pen.

Chapter Two

Meanwhile, the little sewing doll ended up in the big dark forest. She saw trees and a variety of green leaves. At that moment Aya decided to sew a dress for Leah. The doll politely asked the trees:

"May I make a gift from your leaves for my best friend?"

The trees bent low in agreement. The wind came to help, it shook the leaves from the branches.

The sewing doll began to collect the leaves. A Red Groundhog crawled out from its hole to help her, followed by a White-bellied Hedgehog who ran up to her and offered needles to work with.

Aya laid out an armful of leaves and made a small knoll for her sewing machine under one of the trees, on which a Spotted Woodpecker lived, who tirelessly pecked at the tree

with its strong beak. The White-bellied Hedgehog rushed around nearby, always ready to present its dark needles to Aya. Now only threads were missing, luckily the doll saw an Earless Spider crawling nearby.

"Please can I have your thinnest, silkiest strings! I want to surprise a certain little girl, she is my friend!"

The Spider was silent. The doll asked again, but the owner of the threads was speechless.

"It has no ears, it can't hear anything," said the Hedgehog. The Spider then suddenly answered.

"Yes, it's true, I have no ears, but there are small hairs on my legs through which I can hear everything perfectly."

"Then why don't you answer?"

"I am thrifty with by threads. Sometimes I'm even forced to eat my damaged threads so that I can weave more spiderweb."

Aya became so sad that the forest-weaver could not stand it:

"All right, take my cobwebs," said the Spider as it began to throw thin, but strong threads to the little sewing doll.

Chapter Three

Thanking everyone, the doll began to attach leaves to other leaves and sew them by hand. Sometimes, the hedgehog's sharp needles pricked her tender fingers to the blood. But she would continue sewing all those leaves on her tiny sewing machine. Despite the pain in her hands, the doll worked enthusiastically and did not notice how the summer had past her by.

Her surprise was ready – it had turned out to be a bright, green silk dress!

Aya wanted to take the present to her friend and head back home, but then she saw yellow and red leaves slowly falling to the ground.

"I have to sew a colorful blanket for Leah!" Thought the little doll.

And again her forest comrades came to her rescue.

The Red Groundhog helped to collect the multi-colored leaves and then went into its den to sleep through the approaching winter.

For her new task, she took more needles from the back of the White-bellied Hedgehog, but after a time this sharp animal rushed back home to sleep soundly during the winter frosts.

The thread spinner – the Earless Spider threw off elastic, silk threads to Aya as he was making a nest of cobwebs to rest upon through the winter.

By the end of autumn, the doll was finishing the gift alone, only the Spotted Woodpecker, without fear of the cold, occasionally pecked at the tree with its strong beak.

Needless to say, the blanket came out with the warmth of the sunny, early autumn mornings, made as a pattern of orange, red and golded leaves!

Chapter Four

Aya was going home, but when it began to snow, she saw graceful six-pointed snowflakes. She thought that maybe she could make some white, light tulle from them for Leah's room.

The magic-doll had neither threads nor needles left. She shouted at the falling crystals:

"Can I make tulle for my best friend Leah from your delicate frosted forms? She will be very pleased! Though I beg of you, please do not melt!"

"That's alright!" The chorus of snowflakes answered. "We will not melt but promise that you will make the most amazing tulle in the world from us!"

"I promise you!" shouted the tireless doll with happiness.

She chained the snowflakes together. Working with crystals required even more patience, but there is a reason

why so much time had to be spent. By the end of the blizzard, only a glittering tulle of extraordinary beauty remained on Aya's hands.

The doll wanted to show all these gifts to her friend, but then she thought that she could make a lovely curtain for Leah's room from the springs flowers and leaves. As it happens every year, at this time, the snowdrops are the first to bloom, then other flowers follow and Aya's forest friends had awakened from their wintery sleep.

By the beginning of the new summer, the artists work was ready. It turned out to be a luxurious green curtain with languid snowdrops and multi-colored flowers. The Spotted Woodpecker, who had become noisy and loud in the spring, stopped in amazement, and didn't peck on a tree for a few hours, looking at the creations of the sewing doll.

The satisfied Red Groundhog and White-bellied Hedgehog made a basket from thin branches, where they put Aya's sewing machine and gifts for Leah.

Chapter Five

The Spotted Woodpecker, picking the basket up with its beak, flew over to the little girl's house. Down below, Aya ran happily whilst trying to keep up with the bird, excited for her overdue reunion. The Woodpecker put the wickered basket with its gifts on the porch. It knocked on the window with its beak and flew away. Leah opened the door and upon seeing Aya, began to shout:

"How dare you to come to me! Go away! I already have my Maya doll who has been with me this whole time, unlike you who's a traitor!"

"At least accept these gifts, in which I put my whole heart and soul..." said the sewing girl, fighting back her tears, turning around before running back into the forest.

When Leah saw the gifts, she understood how hard Aya had tried for her! These amazing gifts smelled of the forest and its freshness. She felt ashamed, and so the girl run after the sewing doll, taking Maya with her.

"Aya, Aya!!" Shouted the little girl. She ran and she ran until suddenly she saw the Red Groundhog, the White-bellied Hedgehog, the Earless Spider, the Spotted Woodpecker and Aya's handicraft on the forest meadow.

"I would have never helped collecting those leaves if I knew that you were going to be so selfish," muttered the Groundhog whilst looking at Leah, displeasedly waging it's short and thick tail.

"If I had known that you were so heartless, I wouldn't have given a single needle..." puffed out the Hedgehog, stamping his little foot on the ground.

"And I wouldn't have given a single string," the Spider whispered and glared at the girl, disappointment in all eight of its eyes.

Chapter Six

Leah cried, listening to all of the hurtful things the forest dwellers had said, she quietly whispered:

"Forgive me... I'm so sorry..."

"Ungrateful..." the Woodpecker grumbled.

Suddenly, Maya the doll sprang up and began to speak.

"Don't say that to Leah! She's a good girl... She just thought that Aya left her, so she got angry. But she remembered her every day, telling me how they used to be friends!"

And sewing doll also stood up for the little girl.

"Ah, my woodland friends, please do not scold Leah. I forgive her because I will never forget how she bathed me, gave me pretty dresses, combed my hair and told me fairy tales every evening."

"Fairy tales?!" The Spotted Woodpecker was surprised. "Then let her tell us one, and if we like the tale, we will forgive her."

The tears dried on Leah's cheeks, and she looked enthusiastically at the little sewing doll.

"Thank you Aya, you are so kind and faithful!" Said Leah as she glanced at the dolls and the wood-dwellers, smiling and saying:

"Now I'm going to tell a tale of friendship."

The wind brought white sheets of paper with colorfully drawn pictures.

"Oh, and who is this, so cute and prickly?" asked the Hedgehog.

"And who is this red and chubby little fellow?" asked the Groundhog in surprise, looking at the drawn picture of himself.

And each of our heroes found their own colourful image.

"Let us gather all this into a real book," offered the girl.

The Red Groundhog began to run around and collect white and colored papers. The Earless Spider threw off a long thread. The White-bellied Hedgehog offered dark needles to sew the pages together. The Tree where Spotted Woodpecker lived, asked the bird to make a book cover from its bark. The sewing doll fastened everything together with her needle and thread and decorated the pages with bright flowers at the edges.

When everything was ready, Leah began to tell the story, and Maya neatly wrote it all down with her little ballpoint pen: "Once upon a time there was a little girl named Leah and her little sewing doll, Aya..."

THE STUBBORN MAPLE LEAF

That yellow-orange time in Autumn had finally come. Many leaves began to fall from the trees. But one stubborn maple leaf was outraged:

"I'm so beautiful, so wonderful. I don't want to fall. I don't want my house, my maple tree to become barren," the rebellious leaf repeated to itself. "I feel happy here. I love that my leg is attached to the branch through which I drink my water. I love that I'm upside down."

"None of us will be left on this tree when winter comes. Everyone is destined to fall," said the other reasonable leaves hanging next to it.

"No," answered the stubborn leaf. "I'll try not to fall."

A week had passed. All the leaves from the tree had almost fallen off. Our leaf was among the remaining few, firmly holding onto the branch with its leg. Seeing this stubbornness, the wind got angry with the maple leaf:

"Oh, how stubborn you are! Are you saying that you are stronger than nature?! I'll show you now!!"

The wind blew with such force that our leaf snapped off and fell onto the sidewalk.

It was in great pain, but it tried not to cry. Nearby on the ground lay other leaves that awaited it:

"Look who's here, and you were saying:

"I'll try not to fall," they joked. "We are destined not only to fall but also to decay on the ground. It's autumn now, then winter will come, after winter, spring will come and new green leaves will appear on the trees."

"I don't want to crumble, because my shape is too beautiful," said our yellow friend and sighed heavily. "I want to look at the new green leaves."

"Whether you like it or not," the sensible leaves told him. "You will decay. We also do not want it to happen, but we cannot resist the natural way of life."

At this time, a little girl was hopping along the sidewalk when she heard a whisper from under her feet. She sat down and examined the fallen maple leaves. They were extraordinary: yellow, orange, red.

She heard the rustle of our leaf and lifted it from the cold sidewalk.

"I beg you, please take me with you! I don't want to die here!" Said the stubborn leaf.

"You are so big, beautiful and yellow! I want you to always be by my side!"

The happy little girl took the leaf home. She glued it to a thin piece of cardboard and placed it under the glass in a wooden frame. She decided to hang it on the wall in her room, opposite the window and next to her best photo. The girl realized that there was no better place for that stubborn one.

Oh, how proud the maple leaf was that it was given such an honorable place! Every day it happily watched the girl and what was happening outside the window in the garden. That yellow-orange time of autumn had passed, and the white winter had come and gone, now only the warm rays of the colorful

spring sun beamed through the window. Oh, how happy the stubborn yellow maple leaf was when it saw the new, green leaves breaking out of their buds.

The girl also wrote a verse for the stubborn leaf on a sheet of her notebook:

My stubborn little maple leaf,
Amazing as you are!
My stubborn little maple leaf,
Stay close, not too far!

You're hanging in the frame,
My close, little yellow friend.
Stubborn can be your name,
I saw you on your slow descend.

I'm very glad you're next to me,
My dear, my maple friend.
My other friends might stay a while,
Just to see you with their smile.

You live with me, my glorious leaf,
Because you have a strong belief,
Look out to the warm, bright spring,
And watch the new leaves gleam and swing!

They have great fun in the garden,
The sun warms all from up above,
I must say, you make me happy,
Stubborn leaf, whom I dearly love!

When the leaf heard such caring words addressed to itself, it turned even more yellow with joy and pride, saying:

"Thank you my dear! You really are the most wonderful girl!"

THE LEGEND OF ISSYK-KUL

(Excerpt from the fairy-tale, 'Bekbolot and the Issyk-Kul Lake')

Once upon a time, there was a Khan. He had a beautiful daughter named Aytolkun, the girl had long and wavy hair, all the girls in those days braided their hair, only Aytolkun let her beautiful curls down. Since her childhood years, she had loved wearing gorgeous blue dresses. She often danced and played in the garden with her friends, and when she danced, all her movements were smooth and graceful.

When she was sixteen, she married a baatyr[1]. According to Kyrgyz customs, the husband's relatives put a headscarf on the beautiful young princess. The headdress was blue, almost weightless, with long fringes around the edges. She loved this headscarf so much that she never took it off.

She happily lived with her husband and gave birth to two strong babies. Her third son, however, was unlike his brothers, he was often sick and capricious. One day she went over to the beshik[2], where her youngest son lay - she looked at him, but he did not move; she listened to him, but he did not breathe.

Aytolkun began to cry and cry, dropping large, beautiful, sparkling tears onto the ground, until there was so much that it filled up and made a lake.

Since then, a lot of water always fills up the lake at that time of year. People say that the two eldest sons of this unusual

---

1 *a baatyr – a hero*

2 *a beshik – a cradle*

woman became the leaders of their tribes, and Aytolkun from her deep sadness she became the water mother of the Kyrgyz people. Therefore, the Issyk-Kul Lake consoles us as a loving and caring mother, and its waves swing us as if we are in a cradle.

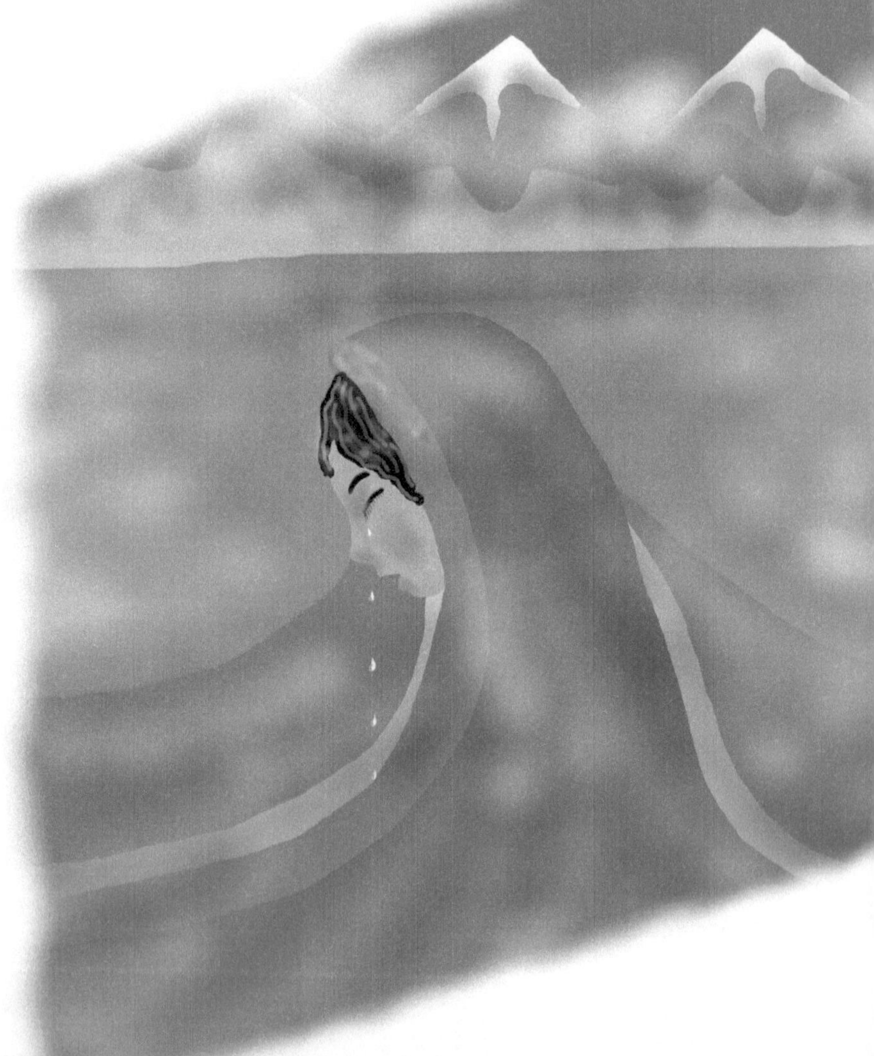

TIEN SHAN, THE TALE OF FOUR SISTERS

Near the Issyk-Kul Lake, there are mountains called the Tien Shan. Four sisters often fly there. Their names are Winter, Spring, Summer, and Autumn.

Winter dresses the tops of the mountains in ice hats, whilst saying:

"I pour snowflakes from the sky and give white blankets to the fields and meadows. My air is fresh and fragrant, especially in the woods. Marmots, hedgehogs, and bears hibernate, for this is a time for these animals to rest.

The kids are happy when my time comes. They are already waiting for me on the hills with sleds to make snowmen and play with snowballs."

Only when Spring comes do the ice hats melt and flow as streams down the mountains to form small lakes. Birds sing, the breeze whispers and various animals run out to play.

"When I come," Spring continued. "The snowdrops timidly look out from under the snows. Animals wake up from hibernation. Rabbits, badgers, and hedgehogs give birth to offspring as more food appears. Birds that had flown away to the south arrive back home. Buds begin to sprout on the trees. The ground gets covered up with grass.

People go out to the fields and vegetable gardens to work and sow the land."

Summer flies in on the mountain, the smell of flowers, medicinal greenery, and fir forests are stretched across the land.

"When my time comes, the trees are lush and green, ripe cherries, apricots, apples, and peaches glister under the scorching sun." Summer says. "You can find different flowers in the meadow. There are poppies, daisies, cornflowers over which the butterflies flutter and bees buzz.

Strawberries begin to slope to the ground, and the scent of raspberries fill the vegetable gardens. Grasshoppers and crickets chirp among the grasses. And after all of that, warm rain pours down as a rainbow appears in the sky.

Seagulls shriek over the lakes and seas because people love to relax in the summer. Joyful children run and play on the shore."

Autumn sighs. Near meadows, burnt herbs appear, rust cold winds shoot through the lands as heavy rain begins its downpour.

"When I come, I paint leaves in orange, yellow, and crimson colors. The birds feast on ripe fruits as they gather in flocks to fly to warmer regions. My favorite flowers are asters, dahlias, and chrysanthemums. People say, 'Chickens are counted in autumn,' meaning this is when people begin their harvest."

Winter, Spring, Summer and Autumn only come when it's their time, but they often meet on the Tien Shan. Therefore, no matter how brightly the sun shines, the tops of the mountains remain icy, and the mountain lakes remain cold.

HUGH THE PEACOCK

The Peacocks live in the wild forest, and among them, there was special one named Hugh. Other peacocks had feathers on their backs just above the tail, forming a multi-colored fan. Hugh didn't have a fan at all, and his upper tail was a bit short.

This saddened him because the other peacocks loved to make fun of his unusual appearance.

"Short-tail!" They would shout. "Not a single female will ever like you, and you will not be able to scare wolves or foxes if you happen to meet them."

The fact is that peacocks, that is, the males, have a luxurious fan of feathers that they need to please the peacock hens, that is, the females. The males also need the tail to scare away animals. If predators see the tail popping out in front of them, they will usually retreat in fear.

Hugh often cried, but no one saw him crying. Before going to sleep Hugh would sit on a tree branch and look at the stars, which he called the "peacock eyes."

"Oh, there are so many of you 'peacock eyes' up there!" He said in admiration. "Oh, fulfill my wish: I want to have the most beautiful tail!"

The stars shone in response but were silent.

When autumn comes, peacocks begin to molt: this is a period when their feathers fall out. Our Hugh decided to pick

up the feathers of the other peacocks and attach them to his own so that he also could have a large and luxurious fan. This task was not easy and required a lot of flexibility and dexterity. He lifted feathers with his beak and twisted them with his paw. It was a funny, yet somewhat sad sight to see.

"Why do you need all those feathers?" Asked Nick, a passing male peacock, in surprise.

"I also want to have a large tail, just like everyone else!"

Nick could not help but feel sorry for Hugh. "Don't worry, I'm sure someone will like you," He tried to console him

Hugh lowered his head and sighed. He didn't want to say that he liked someone, a beautiful female which he saw from time to time, a peacock named Sue.

"Now try to fold your new tail!" Suggested Nick.

Hugh couldn't fold his feathers, but it didn't upset him. "This is actually pretty great! Now I can always walk around with a big loose tail!"

The now happy Hugh returned home with a new tail, but then his mother asked in surprise:

"What have you done son?! You don't look like yourself!"

"I have become like the other peacocks! Now none of the other peacocks will call me names.

"Though I'm not used to this appearance, I'll love you no matter what you look like," his mother smiled.

Hugh loved going to the peacock school, which was located on a flowering lawn. He especially liked it when his teacher, Mr. Pavlinuch, read them fairy tales or taught them mathematics.

In the classroom, all the peacocks tried to sit quietly, they only opened their tails when they wanted to answer.

And since Hugh always sat with his tail loosed out, the teacher asked him more often than others.

Noticing this, his classmates began to be indignant:

"Why is your tail always spread?! You think you're the smartest, or what?! Do you think you can surpass everyone in your studies?!"

"Hey, Hugh, why are pestering everyone with your tail!" Shouted Duke the bully.

"It's not even his tail!" The others laughed. "All those feathers had been screwed on! Duke, look closely, maybe you can find your feathers! Ha-ha!"

Hugh could hardly hold back his tears. They would have continued to laugh it wasn't for Mr. Pavlinuch stopping the class.

"Why is everyone laughing?! Hush, stop making fun of Hugh!"

When Hugh was returning home, Duke met him and blocked his path.

"Come on, don't try flying, jump over my tail instead! I dare you!"

"Easy! Your tail is not so big!" Hugh could not back down and decided to stand up for himself for the first time and rushed at Duke.

They began to bounce, peck, and beat each other with their wings so hard that all of Hugh's feathers fell off completely. But he became more agile, faster, and easily dodged all of Duke's attacks, whose movements became slower due to his heavy tail.

Unexpectedly, even for himself, Hugh emerged victorious. Duke stood before him - exhausted and beaten.

"Sorry Duke! Are you hurt?"

"No, everything is okay."

"I didn't want to fight, but you started first."

Then the beautiful Sue ran over to them:

"Oh, Duke you're always pestering everyone. That's what happens! I hope you don't bully others anymore!"

And turning to Hugh, she said:

"Let's go home together. On the way, I will show you my favorite spots around this place. I especially love the nearby birch forest."

Duke was taken aback by surprise, firstly, his beautiful plumage did him a disservice, and he could not resist Hugh because of his bulky tail. Secondly it turns out, that the most beautiful female in their class liked Hugh.

"Hugh and Sue sitting in a tree…" Muttered Duke as they left.

Hugh and Sue didn't hear him anymore, they were talking as they walked down the path. Sue was joking, and the peacocks laughed, forgetting about the fight.

That night Hugh couldn't sleep on his tree branch for a long time, he was thinking about his life:

"For a while now, I walked around with those strapped-on feathers, but why?! It is much more convenient without them; I think I'm better just the way I am! Probably, every bird, every animal is much more beautiful in their own ways!"

The stars shone in response as if tacitly agreeing as Hugh fell asleep, surrounded by the "peacock eyes".

THE TALE OF THE SCARLET ROSE

Near the small brick house in a flower garden, belonging solely to an old Grandmother, a luxurious Scarlet Rose grew among the pale pink and purple peonies.

The Rose knew about its royal beauty and therefore didn't communicate with the other flowers. The poor peonies either only talked to each other or admired it silently.

Most of all, the White Peony admired the Rose's stately and brilliant beauty. It tirelessly inhaled her aromas, sighed heavily, and yet couldn't bring itself to speak a word.

Once, on a scorching July morning, a Bug sat on the red beauty and quietly murmured:

"Oh, Scarlet Rose, you are so sweet-smelling and tender... May I be your friend? I will fly here every day, then sit on the edge of these velvet petals and enjoy your beauty."

"How dare you offer your friendship to me! Tiny Bug, I am the ruler of all flowers! You have the audacity to bother me? My day was already going badly, and you've just made it worse! "

"Why?!" The insect was surprised.

"Yesterday the wasps and bees came to sit on me! They gathered my pollen and drank my nectar! Those terrible bugs!!"

Their conversation was heard by the wasps and the bees, they came buzzing from every side:

"Oh, Scarlet Rose, you are so greedy,

We'll sting your petals, make it speedy!

Don't you know that from nectar we make sweet honey,

This stuff is very good for you, makes you healthy and funny!

To you proud Rose, we say – Goodbye!

For the little bug, we say: – Just fly away, fly!"

Hearing such words, the Rose got angry, but it didn't have time to answer anything because at the same time, the Grandmother came up to the flowerbed and neatly cut the beauty of the garden.

The elderly woman carried the flower in one hand, along with a soccer ball in the other, she was visiting her grandson for his birthday.

The boy was pleased with the ball, but when he saw the plant, he began exclaiming with displeasure:

"I'm not a girl you know! Don't give these pointless flowers!"

However, the Grandmother carefully put the flower in a vase with some water and said:

"Oh, my dear child, you just don't understand how amazing this Rose is. If you take care of it in the next ten days, it will be a delight for the eyes and soul."

As soon as the Grandmother left, the boy said:

"A soccer ball is cooler! I've always wanted to have one!"

But suddenly, he smelt the delicate scent of the flower. He went up to it and wanted pick it up and smell it more intently. Unfortunately, the sharp thorns of the Rose pricked his fingers.

Out of anger, he immediately threw the poor flower through and out of the balcony.

The poor Rose fell onto the ground and lying there, indignantly thought:

"How could he do that?! What a wicked little boy! He didn't appreciate my beauty, as if I was nothing and a nobody!"

The beauty of flowers was so upset that it wept. It remembered the pale pink and purple peonies:

"Oh, my dear neighbors in the flower garden, now I pity the fact that I never bothered to talk to you. Oh, poor White Peony, it always looked at me so faithfully," said the Rose, sighing heavily.

"The wasps and the bees got angry at me for a good reason, I also broke that tiny Bug's heart with my inattention. I felt so worthless when I was at the little boy's home, thrown away in arrogance like I had done to others, perhaps this is fate..."

The Rose was in though until a little girl picked her up under the balcony.

"Oh, you look so wonderful, but why are you sad?! I see tears on your petals..."

The flower was hesitant but eventually whispered:

"I feel warmth from your tender hands."

The Rose was placed into a thin crystal vase with sugar water in the girl's room for more than a week. Before it faded forever, the Rose said its final words to the girl:

"My dear friend, I want to say that I was happy even though it's only been a few days. If I had previously known how good it is to have a friend, I would have enjoyed my life in the flower garden. Please remember to always appreciate friendship and the ones that care for you the most."

BEKTEMIR AND THE OAK LEAF

Bektemir loved to look out of the window at the oak that grew underneath. He often drew trees and had a variety beautifully different leaves in his drawings. Today, when the boy opened the window, an Oak Leaf decided to talk to him.

"Hello, Bektemir! Are you surprised that I know your name? Don't worry, I am your neighbor after all, and I noticed that you are often very sad."

"Oh, I thought I was the one watching the leaves swing in the breeze. It turns out that you were the one spying on me this whole time?"

"I confess that I am curious and have long dreamed of getting to know you better."

"I never thought that the leaves would one day want to talk to me."

"I have wanted to talk to you for long time now. Tell me, what do you want the most?"

"I want to run and jump in the street, just like the other boys and girls. I am tired of sitting in a wheelchair."

The leaf pondered and then decided to try and dispel Bektemir's sadness.

"Come on, I'll tell you about myself."

"Is your life really that interesting?!"

"I'll guess you'll find out. You see, I have a large family, many brothers and sisters, all living on one single branch. There are many types of leaves: talkative and noisy ones, silent and timid ones, ones that play with the wind and try evading it. I think there are probably hundreds of thousands of leaves on this tree. On these days in May, we whisper and tell each other fairy tales. We also love to warm our bodies in the sun. And now, tell me about yourself!"

"I used to be a healthy kid, but two years ago, my legs and my joints stopped working. My parents took me to different doctors. I spent a long time in the hospitals and drank a lot of medicine, but nothing helped me. At first, I just stumbled, and then I ended up in a wheelchair. Before that I knew how to run, jump, even learned to play football."

"Don't be sad," the Oak Leaf encouraged him. "Are you going to school still?"

"Yes, of course. I'm taught by good teachers and I spend my breaks talking to my classmates. They treat me very well and help me with everything. I have a friendly class, but I can't play like I used to before," the boy said, tears welling up in his eyes.

The Oak Leaf quickly changed the subject.

"Bektemir, do you know where acorns come from? Look at the oak tree: what do you see except for the branches and leaves?"

"I see thin dangling earrings."

"These earrings, oddly enough, are the male flowers. The female flowers take the form of a small green seed with a reddish top. Look, they are on those thin stalks over there, and acorns ripen from them during autumn."

"I like drawing different acorns and pinecones. I can do them beautifully. I love art and I hope that I can become an artist, who knows. But before, I dreamed of being a football player," the boy sighed.

"But you can easily become a sports commentator."

"That is true, I never thought about that before..."

"I have two dreams," the Leaf said. "I achieved one, I wanted to meet you. My other dream is this: I want to break away from this twig and fly away like a butterfly or a bird."

Bektemir's mom entered the room and looked around:

"I heard you talking, is there someone here?"

The boy smiled and replied:

"I'm talking with a funny Oak Leaf."

"I see it cheered you up."

"Yes, can you imagine, mum, it told me where acorns come from, and in general, it also has dreams, just like me."

"Okay, my little dreamer, let's go eat. I cooked some delicious manti."

After dinner, Bektemir went to the garden in his wheelchair. He wanted to quickly get to the oak tree where his new friend hanged. Bektemir got near the lower branch that hang in front of the window of his room. But where was the friendly, talkative Leaf?

"Bektemir, I'm here!" Shouted the Oak Leaf. "Do you feel like the wind is blowing stronger? I think the weather is changing."

"I love the wind, and I love the rain!"

"Me too! Look, I'll try rushing with the wind! Oh, how tightly I am attached to the branch. I need to try a little harder."

"What are you doing?! You can't do it that way!" Shouted the rest of the leaves on the tree.

However, the Leaf decided not to listen to anyone. It stubbornly wanted to get away from the branch and fly into the sky. Finally, it detached himself from the oak tree and flew into the air.

"Look, Bektemir, I'm floating! My wish has been granted!"

The Oak Leaf flew, playing in the air, curling up and straightening its body. It would twist and turn, straighten its posture, roll over, and dance happily.

The boy sat and admired his new friend's freedom with fascination, and at that moment, without even realizing it, he even moved his legs a little. Yes, he managed to move them a little bit.

"My legs moved! I will try to exercise every day. My dad said that if I train hard, I will be able to get on my feet!"

At that moment, Bektemir's mother stepped out into the garden to look for her son.

"What a sudden, strong wind! Hurry home! A downpour will start any minute now, and maybe even a thunderstorm!"

"Mum, wait! Look how beautifully that Oak Leaf is flying!"

"Where? That one? Wow, isn't that great!"

"Do you see it mum?!"

"Yes, I see that it looks like it's trying to wave to you, it looks so happy!"

"I promise Mom and I will no longer be sad because I can still play Legos, study, sing, draw and much more! If I wanted to, I could even become a football commentator or artist, that makes me happy! Hurray!"

"How many times have I told you this and yet you didn't

believe me."

The next day Bektemir looked out of his window and did not see the Oak Leaf on the tree, knowing this was for the best, he whispered:

"Thank you, buddy, you taught me a lot. Why should I be sad? I better go and train. My legs can already move slightly. So, let's see, where was that special exercise book that the doctor gave me?"

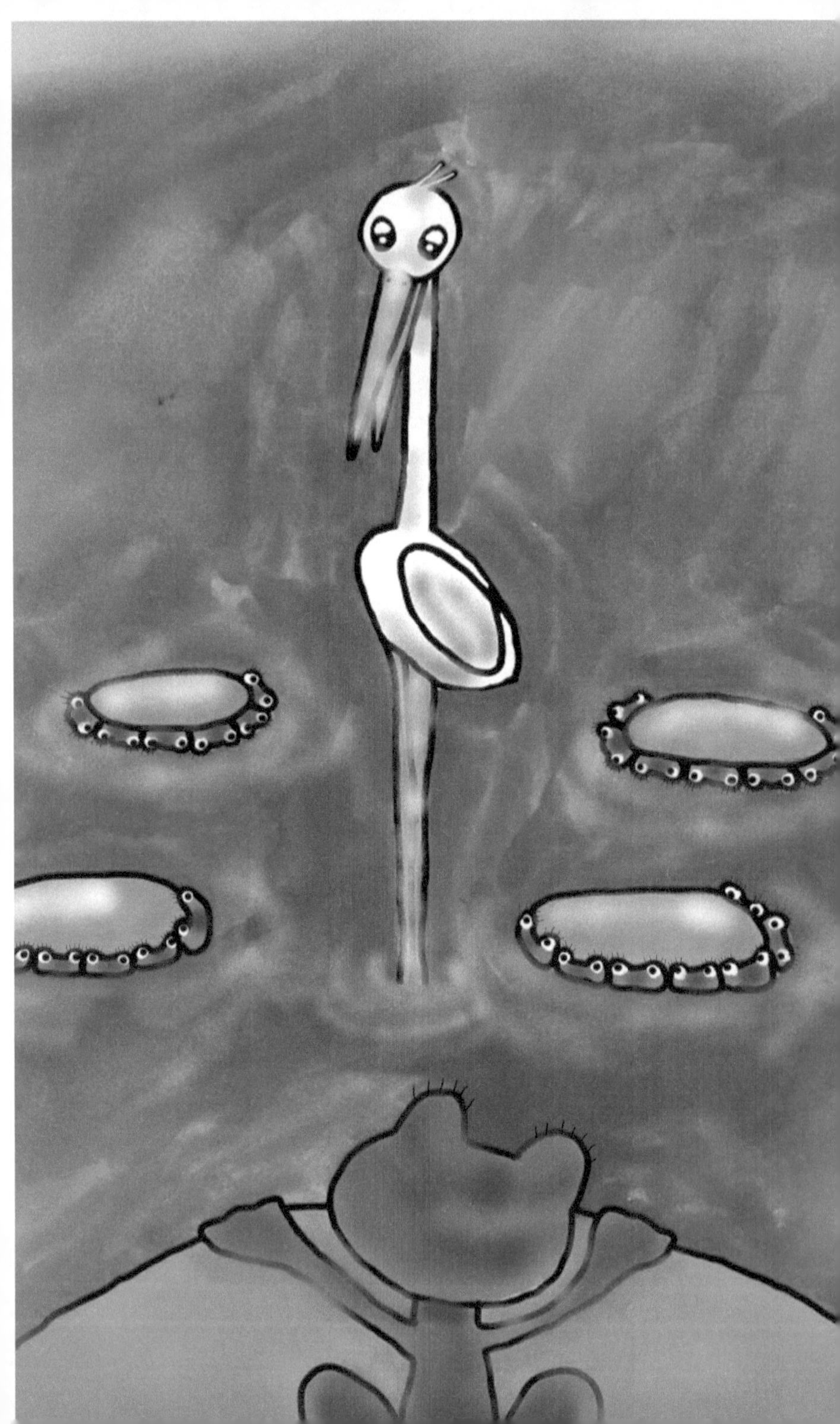

ONCE ON THE SWAMP

During springtime all of the frogs wake up in the swamp, they begin to jump and croak. The Little Frog also woke up. He rejoiced in the spring sun:

"Kwaa-kwaa - what a beautiful day!"

The Little Frog saw a Stork flying straight for the swamp:

"Look, a big white bird is flying towards us!"

The startled Old Frog shouted back:

"You silly Little Frog! That's trouble flying straight towards our swamp..."

"Kwaa-kwaa... But why is it trouble? The bird is so beautiful!"

"The Stork has arrived..." answered the nearby Toad. "If he's heading towards us frogs – then it's truly unfortunate, after all, he devours our kind without any regret."

Realizing the danger of the approaching threat, the Little Frog croaked over the whole swamp:

"Save yourselves if you still can! A dangerous bird is approaching!"

The Stork landed on the edge of the swamp and stood upright, after a short while it fell asleep because it was exhausted from its tiring flight. It slept standing on one leg, and it could not swap its legs without waking up. After awakening, the Stork went to the center of the swamp, where the frogs lived.

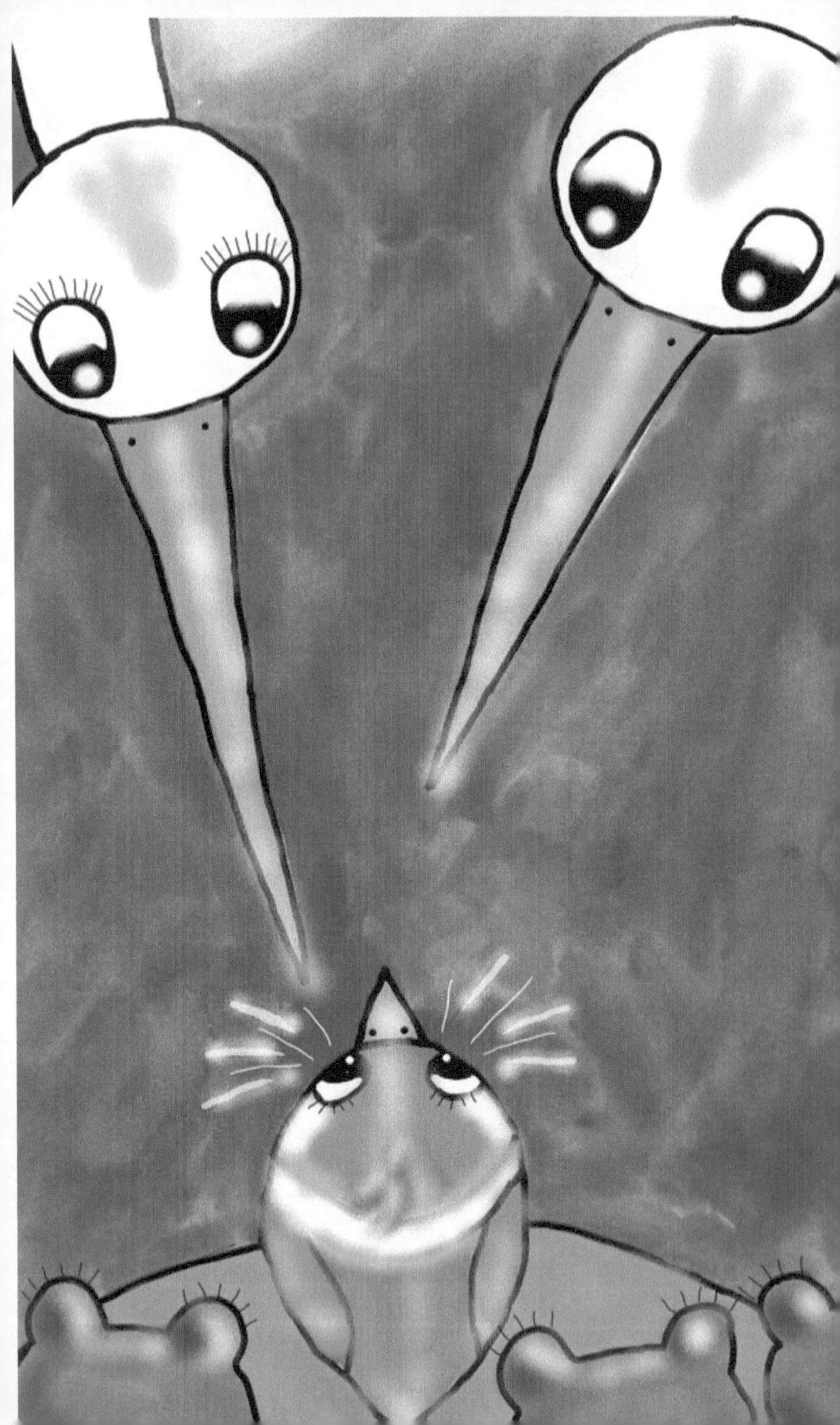

Hearing the footsteps of the Stork, all of the frogs jumped into the water whilst the toads buried themselves in the ground. Both the frogs and toads lay absolutely still, listening carefully to the Stork with their exceptional hearing.

"You've all hidden, hmm. Oh, what difference does it make, you can't go anywhere even if you tried."

Said the Stork confidently.

"How many of you are there in this swamp? Probably around a hundred? To be full for the day, I need to eat ten frogs. So, we divide a hundred by ten to make ten! Which means, that in just ten days, I can eat every last frog in this swamp! Wait a minute, why am I counting only for myself? Soon the Little Stork will arrive, and it will also eat ten frogs a day. So, we divide a hundred by two, that'll be fifty. And fifty divided by ten is five! Oh, we can eat all of them in just five days! We will deal with them very quickly, but what should we eat after? Alright, there are still the fish and worms in store for us I guess," decided the Stork and took refuge in the reeds.

Soon the frogs jumped out onto the land, and the toads got out of the ground, but their fear of the big bird did not leave them.

"What do we do? We must save ourselves," said the Toad.

"Kwaa-kwaa... Let's go to our friend the Sparrow for some advice," offered the Little Frog.

"What can the Sparrow do against that Stork?"

"I don't know, but he's smart, he'll figure something out."

After listening to the complaints of the Toad and the Little Frog, the Sparrow said:

"I have an idea!"

The Toad called the whole frog family, and so a hundred

frogs, led by the Sparrow, fearlessly headed towards the Stork. By that time, the Little Stork had also arrived.

The Sparrow walked in front of everyone. He lamented and cried:

"I used to be Stork you know, but then one day I ate a frog from this damned swamp, then I turned into this pathetic little Sparrow. I was told that this swamp is cursed, but I didn't believe it, I thought it was a fairy tale! Now it's hard to imagine that I was once a big white bird!"

After hearing the Sparrow's story, the Stork turned in shock and said to the Little Stork:

"This Sparrows' situation sounds awful!"

The Little Stork agreed:

"Yes, what a strange and scary story, who knows how awful it would be for us to turn into sparrows! Better we fly to another swamp!"

Together, they flapped with their wings and flew away. They never returned to the swamp because not a single stork ever wants to be a sparrow.

The Little Frog, the Toad and the Sparrow were delighted that their plan had worked. The whole frog family croaked joyfully because the danger had passed.

The Sparrow modestly chirped:

"The Storks, are of course, big, white and beautiful, but being a Sparrow isn't so bad."

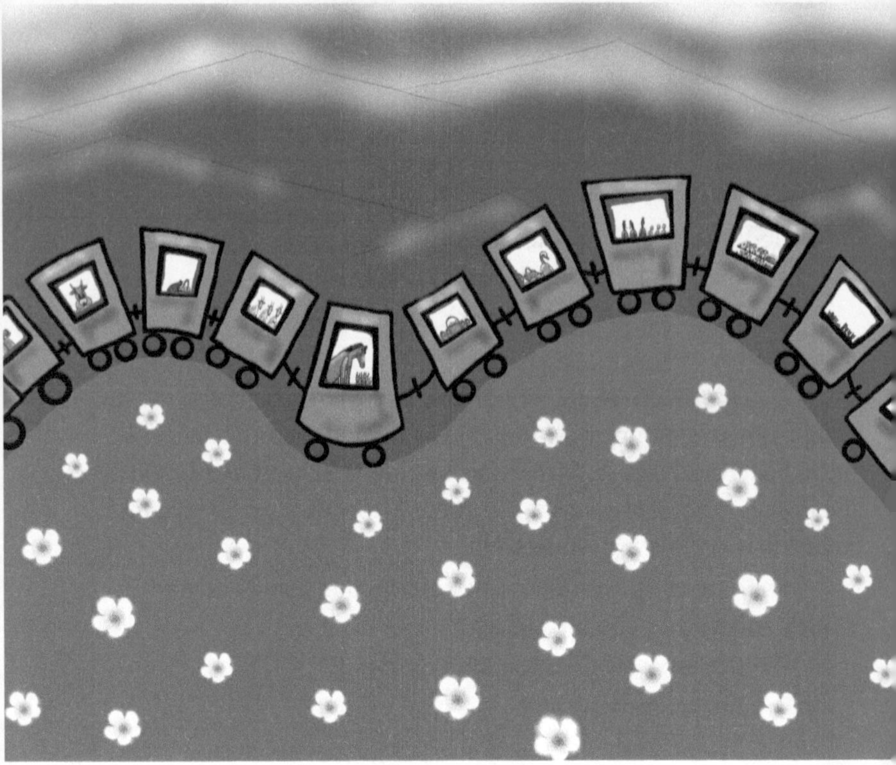

TEN WAGONS

The train with ten wagons ran across the tracks. There were different animals and birds in those wagons. How about we take a look at some of them.

There was the Cow in the first wagon. She was alone, only a two-liter can of milk and a bowl with ten kuruts (a dry sour milk product) stood way in the back of the wagon. In all honesty, the Cow was bored of being alone, so she decided to visit those who were traveling in the second wagon.

In the second wagon there were two hens. Their baskets filled with eggs.

The Cow squeezed between the wagons and approached the hens.

"May I stay with you two?"

One of the hens didn't mind, but the one with the brown feathers and the red comb said:

"Dear Cow, please don't be offended, but you are way too big, it will be cramped for us in here. You can stay if you really have to, though I myself will leave and see who's in the third wagon."

The third wagon had three Goats, and each of them had a liter of milk in a can as well as twelve kuruts in three separate bowls.

"Oh, looks like the Brown Hen has come to see us... Come

in, make yourself at home, you're our guest after all."

"No, I don't want to be your guest, may I just stay with you? The Cow came to our wagon and took up a lot of space with her big body."

The Goats looked at each other, and the eldest asked:

"Who else is in the second wagon?"

"Another hen."

"Well, that hen is not an elephant, is she? There should be enough space in that wagon, you are just being greedy."

The Brown Hen was offended and left the third wagon.

She entered the fourth wagon and saw the Horse and three Squirrels. The Squirrels were gnawing at nuts. There was a full bowl of koumiss (a drink made from mare's milk) and a bowl of kuruts near the Horse.

"That's interesting - all of you have kuruts: the Goats, the Cow, and you too wise Horse?" Said the Brown Hen in surprise.

"Well, kuruts can be made from cow's, goat's or mare's milk," answered the Horse.

"Will you treat me to your kuruts? I want to live here with you because the Cow came to our second wagon as an uninvited guest."

"How about you? Did one of us invite you over?" One of the Squirrels asked.

"I see how it is! At least I don't take up so much space!" The Brown Hen said in disappointment and went to look for a place in another wagon.

The fifth wagon had five cute Hedgehogs. Next to them, there was a basket of large apples and mushrooms.

"Hello," said the Brown Hen. "You are so small and cute-looking. Can I be friends with you?"

"Frr-frr," answered the roundest of the Hedgehogs. "Just show us your ticket and you're welcome to stay."

"I don't have a ticket. I'm from the second wagon but I left because the big Cow came and took up all the space."

"Frr-frr, then the Cow should simply go back to its own wagon and you should go to yours. Otherwise, the Turkey-Conductor that is checking the wagons will come here and fine us."

"Oh, how inhospitable you are!"

The Brown Hen entered the sixth wagon, where the Large Duck and the White Goose were sitting. There were two baskets of eggs on the table nearby.

"There are only two of you," the Brown Hen sighed in relief. "I finally found a place to stay."

"What's the matter?" The White Goose asked with a frown.

"You see…" And the bird began to tell them her story.

"Just go back to your wagon," the Large Duck whispered sternly. "I think that Cow has already left, she probably just wanted to meet you and talk, I don't think she wanted to stay there and bother you."

However, the Brown Hen did not stop her search.

"Somewhere here there has to be a kind animal..." The Brown Hen reasoned with herself and entered the seventh wagon.

There she saw the grand Peacocks and three Pheasants sitting on fancy little chairs.

"Wow, you really are beautiful birds!"

"Who are you?" Asked the Peacock with the largest tail.

"I am a close relative of yours from the Pheasant side of the family."

"Ha-ha-ha, you silly little Brown Hen, you don't look like us at all," the Peacocks with the largest tail remarked as they all giggled.

The Brown Hen was again offended and sighed.

"Why don't they recognize the obvious..."

The Brown Hen stood in the passage of the train and almost cried.

"It makes no sense to go to the eighth, ninth and tenth wagon. Nobody here accepts me. It would be better to go back to my wagon and make friends with the Cow."

The Brown Hen did not enter the eighth wagon, where the eight Rams were traveling with two chests full of wool.

She did not enter the ninth wagon, where there were four Cats and five Dogs.

She decided to return to the second cabin.

Then suddenly a voice came from the train announcement speakers: it was the Turkey-Conductor who loudly called for all of the animals to gather in the tenth wagon.

"The Guinea-Pig is waiting for you all, she is inviting all of the birds and animals in the train to her birthday party!"

The Brown Hen ran to get her eggs, the Cow for her milk. In general, all the animals were alarmed and hurried all over the place to prepare their gifts.

After a few minutes, the animals and the birds gathered at the Guinea-Pig's wagon. Although the tenth wagon was the most spacious, it was still amazing how everyone was able to fit in there. The two hens sat on the Cow, the three Squirrels on the Horse, the five Hedgehogs sat on the Large Duck and

the White Goose. The Pheasants and Peacocks sat on the Rams and the Cats on the Dogs. All of them were cheerfully going towards the Issyk-Kul Lake and they were celebrating the Guinea-Pig's birthday on the way. They ate an apple pie, some kuruts and a large round loaf with milk and koumiss. Everyone brought gifts and treats.

"I've never had so many gifts before!" The Guinea-Pig gleamed with joy.

There was a list of gifts. If you want – we can count them together. Better to count all of the gifts separately, to see who brought what.

The Cow: two liters of milk and ten kuruts.

The Hens: ten eggs each.

The three Goats: a liter of milk each and twelve kuruts each.

The Horse: a bowl of koumiss and a dozen kuruts.

The two Squirrels: seven cones each.

Two Hedgehogs: fourteen apples each, three Hedgehogs: thirteen mushrooms each.

The Large Duck: six duck eggs.

The White Goose: eleven goose eggs.

The three Peacocks: each with seven feathers, the three Pheasants: six pheasant eggs.

The eight Rams: two full chests of wool.

The Dogs and Cats were the only ones that did not know what to bring. But they made up for it with their own type of gift: jokes, anecdotes, and entertainment.

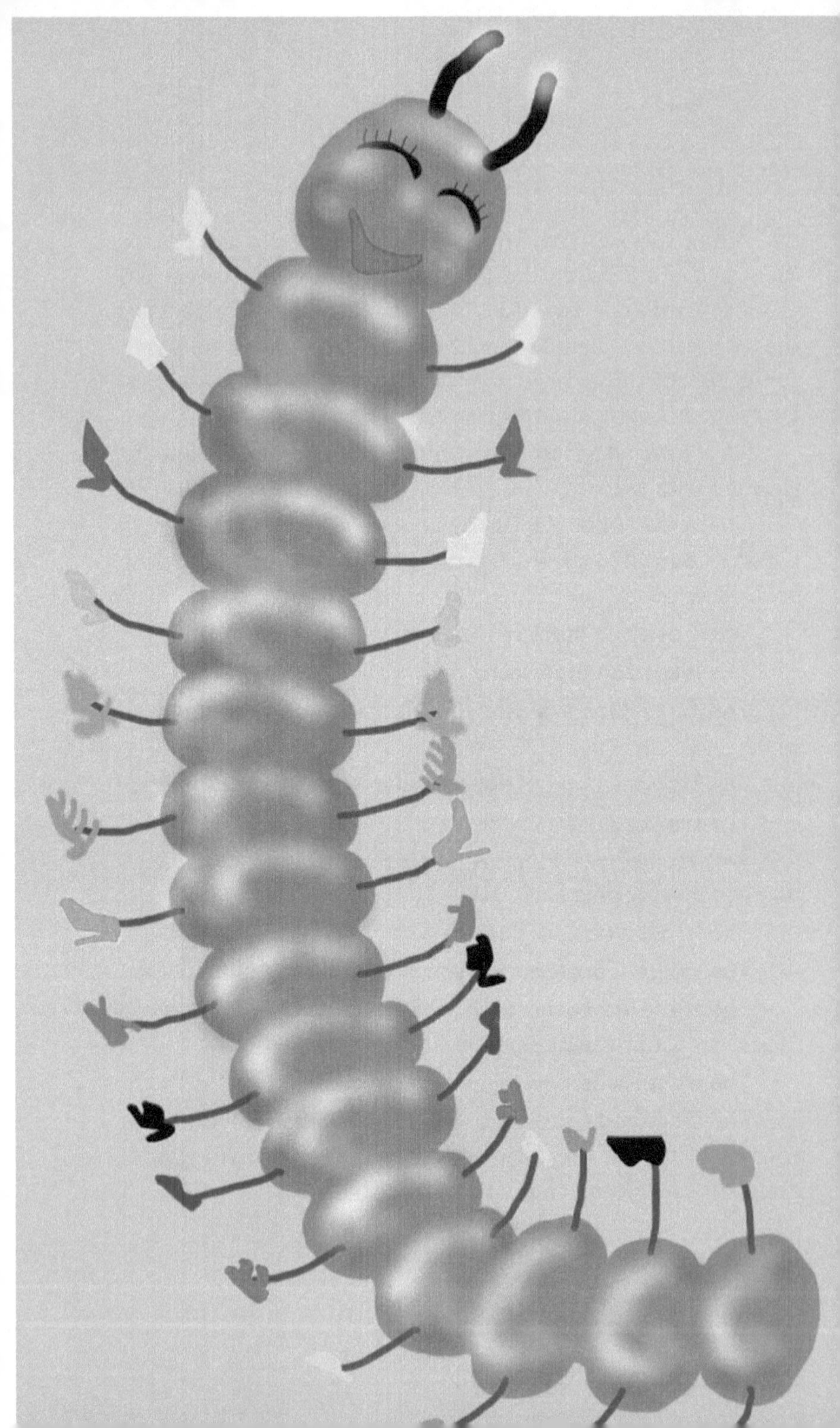

Ozhka the Centipede

A family of centipedes lived in a small damp basement. These centipedes were sometimes called the flycatchers, their family consisted of the father, who was a worker, the mother who was a housewife, and their many, many children. The smallest of these children was called Ozhka.

Almost every day, the centipede children would run out onto the porch of a huge house and see a human woman with her son. The Mother would take the boy out for a walk and on their way out, she would repeat to him:

"Oh, my dear little son, are you ready for our walk?"

The centipede children wondered how he can be little if he was so big.

One day, Ozhka saw the human mother putting boots onto her son, tying the long shoelaces in a knot before walking off. Then Ozhka looked at her bare legs and thought:

"Why won't mum and dad buy me any shoes or boots... Now, if I had boots and sandals, I would be the happiest centipede in the world!"

The little centipede got upset and ran into the dark basement, huddled in a corner and rubbed her small tears with her feet.

"What happened Ozhka, why are you crying?" Her parents asked her.

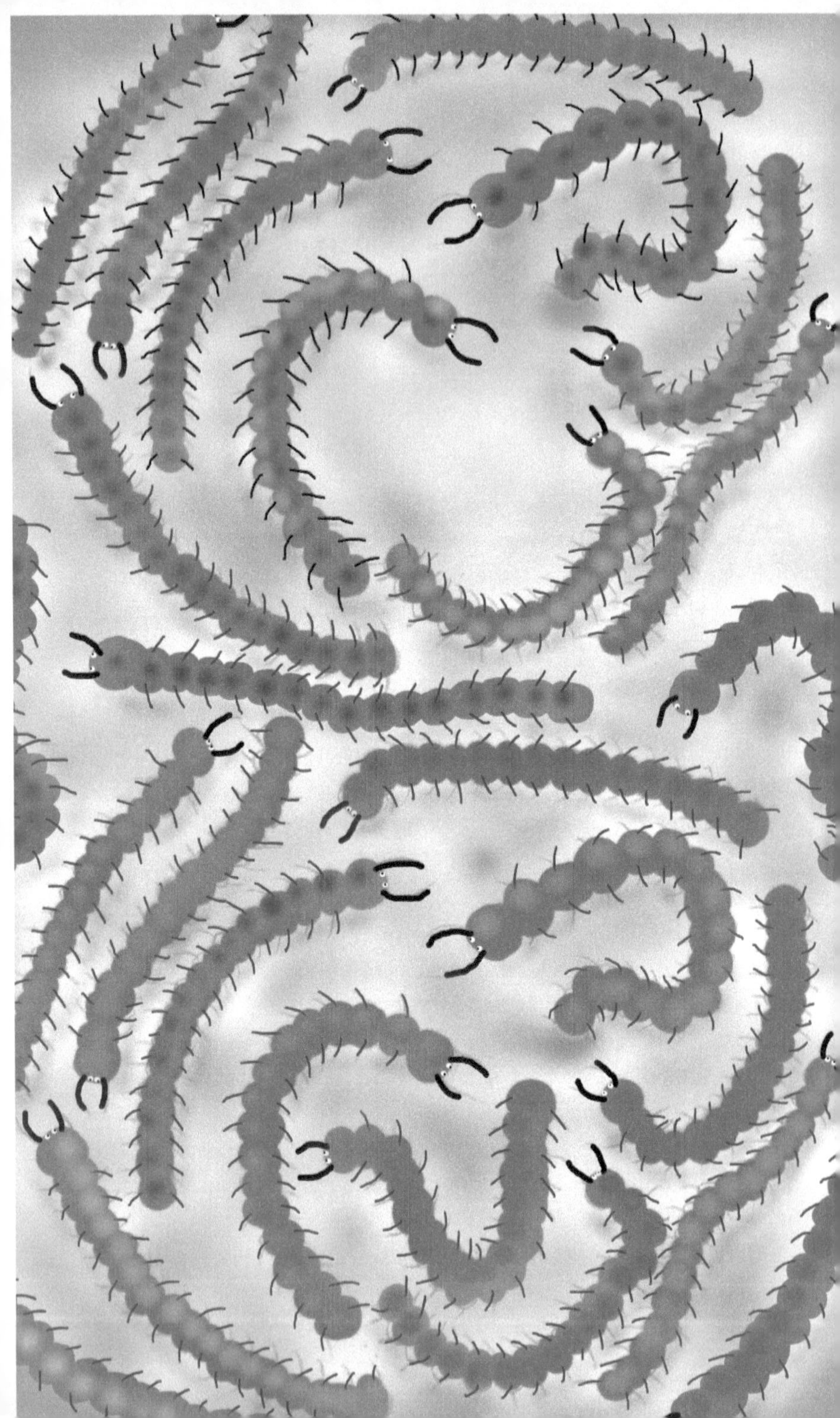

"Because you won't buy me any shoes," she said, and began to cry more.

"Oh Ozhka, just count how many legs you have, where will we find that much money!" Exclaimed the mother.

Ozhka managed to count up to twenty before losing count.

"You have thirty legs, so you need fifteen pairs of shoes! Trying to acquire them is a waste that we cannot afford!" Sternly said the mother, who did not like the little centipede's idea.

However, the father decided to support his favorite daughter.

"I've been saving up money for three years.They are at the Millipede Bank. Don't cry my daughter, I'll buy you whatever you want."

The father ran to the bank and withdrew the money from his account, then he went shopping with Ozhka. When they arrived, they saw that there where shoes for beetles and caftans for grasshoppers.The shop owner was a red cockroach.

Oh, how the centipede's eyes lit up at the sight of pretty shoes on the counters!

"Dad, please buy these pink ones!" Demanded Ozhka.

The cockroach slyly looked at them and realized that such customers rarely entered his shop.

"If you only get this pair, you will still remain barefoot, ask your father if he would be kind enough to get these too, it's my recommendation," the cockroach handed golden sandals with long bootlaces to Ozhka.

The father nodded approvingly, less than half an hour later, the shoe racks were empty. Only the grasshopper caftans remained on the hangers. The cockroach was incredibly happy, but Ozhka's father was saddened because there was no money left at all.

"Are you satisfied now?" asked the father.

"Yes, thank you very much, though four of my legs are still barefoot, it will be cold and uncomfortable without two more pairs of shoes."

"My dear, all of the shelves are empty and so is my wallet."

In joy, the cockroach decided to surprise them. He ran to his warehouse and brought one pair of warm felt boots and another pair of summer slates:

"You bought several pairs of expensive shoes from me, so I'll give these boots and slates to you completely free of charge."

Ozhka stood in front of the mirror at the shop, admiring herself. Boots, sandals, felt boots... they all looked so pretty. Her legs seemed more beautiful than they've ever been. Her mood was so high that she would have gladly jumped up and shouted out in joy, however, there was a problem.

It soon turned out that outside of just jumping or running, even crawling around became very inconvenient. After all, these shoes were sold for beetles, but for Ozhka they were way too big. The caprice girl could barely move, her father slowly crawled beside her with his bare feet, realizing that he was left without a penny, he already regretted not listening to his judicious wife.

When they crawled into the basement, Ozhka's indignant brothers and sisters surrounded her from all sides.

"We want shoes too! All of us need shoes!" They shouted.

"Alas," replied the father. "I've already spent all my money.

I have nothing left."

The brothers got angry at Ozhka:

"Dad is bankrupt, are you happy now?!"

"Why did you spend so much money?" The mother asked the father indignantly. "You spent all of that saved money on only one daughter when we have twenty-five children in our family!"

The father felt ashamed:

"I give you my word - next time, I will consult you when it comes to large purchases, and I will respect whatever your opinion might be."

The sisters looked at her legs with envy, but soon everyone wanted to play outside because the rain had passed. The ground was wet, and the centipede children liked it that way. They ran and began to play tag and hide-and-seek, Ozhka was the only one that had to drag her legs with difficulty.

"These are such stupid shoes," she thought. "They are no use at all. What a pity that I ended up wasting my father's money that he had been saving up for three years."

Then a grasshopper in a green caftan flew up to her, sat down on a green blade of grass so that he could not be seen, and began talking to her:

"Oh, you centipedes are all so similar, how do your parents distinguish you apart?"

"Similar?! Mom and Dad say that we are very cute and different."

"Well tell me, are your legs also very cute and different?"

"They are all very different, all thirty of them!"

"Oh, I see," The grasshopper continued to tease her. "You know, this is the first time I have ever see such a strange

centipede. Look how everyone else is having fun, and you? You can barely move those 'different' little legs."

Ozhka did not say anything, she just threw her shoes off her feet in frustration and ran to play with her siblings, completely barefoot.

As for the grasshopper, after spreading his wings, he uttered:

"I guess that's just life, just business and just whimsy little children!"

The Dolphin Boy

Chapter One

One day a young mother went to bathe her newborn son in the sea. She was sure that the azure waters would make the baby hardened and strong.

"Oh, my dear boy, may the sea spirits make you strong and handsome," she uttered.

The sun generously shared its rays, and a light breeze was blowing. The mother carefully held the little body in the gentle waves. The sea spirits that are invisible to the human eye filled the boy with strength.

But in an instant, her son disappeared from her hands. There was actually a Cunning Shark, watching, lurking in the water. The Shark sharply knocked the baby out of her mother's hands with its tail. The Shark wanted nothing more than to devour the child, but fortunately the Dolphin Dean, who was well aware of the Shark's cruel intentions, was swimming nearby.

The mother of the newborn baby was wailing heavily on the shore, her hot tears running down her cheeks. She was running along the shore, rushing further and further into the sea, when she was exhausted from swimming, she swam back onto the land. After collapsing on the shore, her heart begun to slow down, she was completely frozen from grief, eventually becoming a stone statue.

At the same time, Dean the lifeguard was supporting the baby in the water as if he was one of his own dolphins. After swimming back to his flock, Dean and the other dolphins begun discussing about what should be done with the boy.

"We mustn't leave him. We will protect him from sea monsters and predators," decided the Noblest Dolphin, that is, the head of the family. "Every day, we will give him our milk and play with him. Let him frolic in the sea and take air baths from time to time."

What can I say, the dolphins loved the boy who could only cry. They took care of him, giving him milk and catching the tiniest fish for him. After a while, the child learned to smile and then to laugh. To him, it seemed to be that he was born in the sea, and so the dolphins gave him the name, Dolphin Boy.

However, the Cunning Shark could not forget what had happened, how it allowed for the boy to escape into the deep waters of the sea. It was waiting for an opportunity to devour the child. Seeing the Cunning Shark's restless state, the Most Terrible One, who was the ruler of all sharks, asked his friend:

"What torments you, my friend?"

"I knocked a newborn boy out of this woman's hands, but that damned dolphin Dean stole my tasty prey!"

The Most Terrible One gathered all of the sharks.

"For you my friend, I will declare war on the dolphins! We must take the boy, by all means! Forward my fellow sharks!"

They swam swiftly towards the flock, without any warning of the attack. The dolphins with the strongest instincts heard the approaching sharks and gathered everyone into one huge flock.

The Most Terrible One began his demand:

"Give us our prey, it is a matter of honor! You have no right to do what you want in this sea!"

To which the Noble Dolphin objected:

"We will not give up the boy, as for you Most Terrible One, I forbid you from hurting humans in general!"

"Who dares speak to me that way?! Who are you to forbid me from anything?! Now that you have angered me, we will fight for life and death."

The Noble Dolphin replied:

"Although I have gathered a huge army, we will fight one on one."

At the same time, the Cunning Shark seized the heat of the moment. When the unsuspecting child emerged from the water, it swam up to him and prepared to devour him, just like the first time.

But something was happening to the sea! The waves raged, and even the sea spirits were angry with the predator. The Noblest Dolphin began to fight with the Most Terrible One. At the same time, several dolphins surrounded the Cunning Shark that wanted to eat the boy.

"If you devour the boy, you lose your head."

The Cunning Shark was frustrated, this was the moment it was waiting for, its tasty prey was right there! But the Shark understood that if it devoured the boy, then it would die. Struggling with this realization, the Shark swam away from the boy, thinking with annoyance:

"Those damn dolphins, if it were not for you, the boy would have been in my stomach long ago!"

The waters darkened and boiled as the Noblest Dolphin fought stubbornly with the Most Terrible One for a long time.

The Terrible One bit down on the Dolphin, drawing out blood and leaving deep wounds on the dolphin's smooth body. They fought with their fins, tails, bodies and muzzles. In the end, the Dolphins were victorious, and the exhausted predators began to beg:

"Leave me, I beg of you, I want to live..."

"On one condition, promise that your whole family will never touch people ever again! Whether it's when the fishermen are fishing, and you tear their nets, scatter their fish, or worst of all, when you attack innocent children. You should just eat jellyfish or fish, but never people!"

"Okay, I promise, just let me live..."

Chapter Two

The Dolphin Boy was growing up. He had fun and played with the dolphins. He loved and acted just like them, jumping high from the sea, making smooth, beautiful circles and then plunging back into the water. He also liked to take water into his mouth and then spray it upward like a fountain. He did it well.

The boy was also empowered with such strength that he could escort ships into the open sea with a flock of dolphins. If he was tired, he sat on the back of one of them and admired his brothers as he rested.

Surprisingly, these sea animals do not sleep, they swim constantly. At night, the Dolphin Boy often lay down on the

Dean and, looking at the stars, fell asleep to the sound of waves and the wind. He was sure he was born in the sea.

And so, a full seven years have passed and one day the Dolphin Boy swam close to the shore and saw a statue. He looked at her for a long time and suddenly burst into tears. This stone woman seemed close and dear to him as if he knew something about her. The child stared at the statue, deep in thought, and at that moment, the Dean swam up to him.

"I have been waiting for this moment for a long time, I guess now it's the time for me to tell you the truth. You are a human and the son to that stone statue, though before, she used to be a living woman," the Dean told him the whole story.

"How can we revive my mother?!"

"Oh, if only I knew, I would have revived her long ago. But, alas, this is beyond my power!"

The Dolphin Boy was troubled after hearing the truth and swam to the shore several times a day. He looked at the motionless woman but could do nothing, until one day, in deep despair, he shouted:

"Oh, sun! Help me with you heat! Bring my mother back to life! Oh, wind! Help me with your strength! Bring my mother back to life!" And after shouting and shouting, the boy collapsed and began to loudly sob.

At that moment, the wave carried him to the shore, where he washed up on the dry land.

The little boy, to his surprise, discovered that he could not only swim but also walk on the ground. He hurriedly walked towards the statue. At that moment, a miracle happened: the fiery sun melted the stone, and the coastal wind blew off the residue, the woman had been revived. After she opened her eyes, she immediately recognized her son and hugged him.

As befits any human, the Dolphin Boy began to study, and after his classes, he always hurried back to his native waters, where he swam for a long time with his Dolphin brethren.

The sea spirits gave him endurance, speed and invincibility that even the sharks shunned him. But he still loved to play and talk with his dolphin brothers and sisters. About what exactly? Nobody knows, maybe he'll us himself someday, we'll just have to wait and see.

www.ingramcontent.com/pod-product-compliance
Lightning Source LLC
Chambersburg PA
CBHW030601310726
48979CB00003B/534

9781913356453